The Good Spy Guide

DISGUISE
& MAKE-UP

W9-CNC-852

Christopher Rawson
Heather Amery
Anita Harper

Colour Illustration:
Colin King
Black-and-white Illustration:
Juliet Stanwell-Smith

About this book

All over the world, there are different sorts of spies living secret lives, and looking for clues and information. This book is full of good ideas for everyone who enjoys playing spy games, and making and wearing disguises.

Follow the adventures of the Good Spies on their secret spying missions. See how they surprise and bluff the Enemy Spies. Learn how to keep watch on buildings without arousing suspicion, and how to hide secret messages in your clothes.

This book shows how to change your appearance with hats, wigs, make-up and other special effects. It explains how to change your voice and your walk, how to keep a scrapbook of good disguise ideas, and how to build up a collection of secret disguises for all missions.

First published in 1978 by Usborne Publishing Ltd
20 Garrick Street, London WC2 9BJ, England

Published in Australia by Rigby Ltd
Adelaide, Sydney, Melbourne, Brisbane, Perth

Published in Canada by Hayes Publishing Ltd
Burlington, Ontario

© Usborne Publishing Ltd 1978

Printed in Belgium by Henri Proost, Turnhout, Belgium.

The Good Spy Guide

DISGUISE & MAKE-UP

Contents

4 Why Disguise?
6 Quick Cover-Ups
8 Decoys
10 Hints and Warnings
12 Detecting Disguises
14 Watching People
16 Secret Mission
18 Spot the Mistakes
20 Spy Challenge
22 Spot the Spies
24 Which Hat?
26 Quick Disguise Collection
28 Check Your Equipment
30 How to Put on Make-Up
34 Special Effects
36 Change Your Walk
38 Making Yourself Look Fat
40 Making Yourself Look Old
42 Secret Hiding Places
46 False Noses
47 Hands and Nails
48 Moustaches
49 Beards
50 Change Your Hair
51 Wigs
52 Hats
53 Scarves
54 Change Your Voice
56 Disguise Scrapbook
60 Spy Spotter's Sketchbook
64 Spy Language

Why Disguise?

Good Spies wear disguises so they will not be recognized by the Enemy Spies. Then they can watch them without being discovered, and keep them guessing by changing their disguises.

Try to avoid being photographed. Then the Enemy Spies will not have a record of your face.

Choose your disguise carefully. Try to wear clothes which help you fit into your surroundings.

When you are out on a spying mission at night

or during the day, act in a way that looks ordinary.

Use cover, such as trees, to keep watch on suspicious-looking people without them knowing.

Change your disguises as often as you can. Then the watching Enemy will not know who is the spy.

Use different tricks to get away from the Enemy. Keep them waiting and watching after you have gone.

Quick Cover-Ups

Your secret spying missions will only be successful if the Enemy spies do not recognize you. Here are a few tricks to help keep your face hidden from them. Always be prepared to take action. You never know where the next Enemy Spy may be.

1 Newspaper Trick

You are out keeping watch on a building when an Enemy Spy comes round the corner.

You carefully raise your newspaper, peeping over the top as the spy comes towards you.

Then out of the corner of your eye you spot a second spy, a few yards behind the first one.

Now you must keep an eye on them both, making sure neither of them can see your face.

When both have passed, you can fold up your paper and follow them to their secret destination.

Always carry a handkerchief in your pocket. Whip it out and use it in an emergency.

An umbrella is another useful piece of equipment for hiding your face in moments of danger.

Pretend to drop some money. But make sure that an Enemy Spy does not try to join in.

If you are carrying a bag or brief case, bend right over and pretend to look for something in it.

In a real emergency, the only way to keep your

face hidden might be to tie your shoelace.

7

Decoys

Enemy spies will feel really safe only if they
are quite sure they know where you are. Here
are some cunning ways to keep them waiting
while you go to your next assignment.

Spies often do their most
secret work at night.
Never leave your bed
unoccupied even when
you are away on a night
mission. Leave a dummy
under the bedclothes to
trick the Enemy Spy.

1 Spy Shadow

This trick shows how to
collect a secret document
from HQ, and escape
without being followed.

2

The spy outside watches
you go in. The light goes
on and he sees your
shadow at the window.

8

1 Who's Watching Who?

Who is the mysterious person behind the garden fence who just goes on watching hour after hour?

Nobody feels safe if they are being watched. Imagine how this spy feels trapped upstairs.

But it is your dummy that sits in front of the window while you prepare to escape.

The Enemy Spy soon gets tired of watching you in your HQ. Now you can slip away into the night.

9

Hints and Warnings

Here are a few ideas that will help you to be a better spy and move about unrecognized when you are out on a secret mission. It is always important to wear the sort of clothes that help you to fit in with your surroundings.

Bright Lights

Always keep in the shadows at night. Avoid the glare of street lights and lighted windows.

Familiar Smells

Beware of dogs that know you. They will recognize you even though you are well disguised.

Bluff

Sometimes you can help a friend to spy by causing a diversion. This attracts the Enemy Spies' attention.

1 Double Bluff

Here's a good trick to try. Two of you dress exactly the same. Hide your faces as you pass an enemy spy.

1 Fitting In

If you are spying on a building that is guarded,

think of a good disguise or you will be spotted.

2

One good way to baffle the Enemy Spies is to wear

the same sort of clothes as local people.

2

When you have passed by, he will be sure to follow, hoping you will lead him back to your HQ.

3

Now you separate and both set off in different directions. He will not know which one to follow.

Detecting Disguises

However good your own disguise is, it is just as important to be able to recognize when other people are in disguise. You will only be prepared for the sort of tricks the Enemy Spies will try to play on you, if you are quite sure they really are spies.

Here are a few ways of checking up on suspicious people. Try them out on your friends at home first, then you will know exactly what to do when you meet a suspect.

1 The Bear Hug

2

See how this Good Spy tests if the lady suspect is a spy too. He rushes up to give her a big hug.

She is so surprised that he is able to feel for padding or secret pockets in her clothes.

12

1 Shockers

If you suspect that a woman is really a man in disguise, give her a shock and listen to the scream.

2

When she turns and runs away, you will easily be able to see if it really is a woman, or a man.

1 Wet Hand Shake

Carry a damp sponge in your raincoat pocket. If a person looks as if he is wearing hand make-up,

2

quickly rub your fingers on the sponge and shake his hand firmly. Some make-up may come off.

False Beard Trick

To get a close look at a suspicious-looking beard, pretend you can see an insect caught in it.

Clean-up

Offer to rub a smudge off someone's face with your handkerchief, if you think they might be disguised.

Watching People

When you are thinking about a new disguise, it is a good idea to spend some time watching other people to see how they behave. But do it carefully. Most people do not like being stared at and some of them might be spies too.

Look at people when they are asleep. Some open their mouths and snore. Others let their heads fall forwards.

People do funny things with their legs when they are sitting down. Some cross them over, others waggle their feet.

Habits

Only very well trained spies are able to change their habits when in disguise. If you watch people waiting at a bus stop, you will see how many different ways there are of just standing and waiting. People's habits become even more obvious when they start moving and doing things. Build up a file of how people behave and practise copying them.

WAITING	WALKING

Watch how people carry things. See if they are used to doing it.

People have different ways of eating. Some hold their knives and forks carefully and eat slowly. Others eat very fast and spill things.

Try looking at people from behind. Back views are difficult to disguise. Which of the two people here might be the man?

RUNNING	STALKING	YAWNING	TALKING

15

Secret Mission

Undercover Agent 9412X (code name Zed) is ordered by Headquarters to collect a file of secret plans. It has been put in a left luggage locker at the International Airport. Zed has been sent the key and warned that the Enemy Spies have been tipped off. They know the file is hidden somewhere in the Airport and are watching, hoping to grab it. Can Zed get the file safely away without being spotted?

ZED GOES TO THE AIRPORT IN A TAXI!...

DISGUISED AS A PASSENGER FLYING TO A FOREIGN CITY.

HE GOES INTO THE TOILET, UNOBSERVED.

QUICKLY HE CHANGES INTO A NEW DISGUISE...

AS A REPAIR MAN WORKING IN THE AIRPORT.

PRETENDING TO REPAIR THE LOCKERS, HE GETS THE FILE.

BACK IN THE TOILET HE PUTS ON ANOTHER DISGUISE...

AND PREPARES TO LEAVE.

SAFELY THROUGH THE DOOR, HE HAILS A TAXI!

THE OPPOSITION ARE PUZZLED, BUT ZED IS SAFE.

17

Spot the Mistakes

The Embassy has invited many special guests to a reception. Presidents and Ambassadors from many foreign countries are there. HQ is tipped off that some Enemy Spies disguised as guests and waiters may try to attend to gather secret information. How many suspicious looking people can you see? There are at least 20.

19

Spy Challenge

This is a spy game for two players. Look at the boxes below to find out how to make the board and stand-up spies. Each player can paint his spies a different colour.

You will need
thick white cardboard
(about 24 cm × 24 cm)
thin cardboard for the
spy stand-ups
a ruler and a pencil
paint and glue
a paint brush

The Board

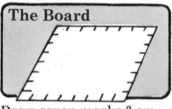

Draw seven marks 3 cm apart along each side of the cardboard. Rule lines from the top to bottom marks and from the sides.

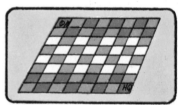

Paint the squares like this. The red squares are the spies home territory. Write HQ on the red squares in two corners.

Spy Stand-Ups

Cut out 16 strips of thin cardboard, each 7 cm × 2 cm. Fold them in half and bend out the ends (a). Glue the two halves (b).

Paint spy faces on one side. On the other side, for each player, draw an M on one stand-up and numbers on the others.

The Game

Each player has seven spies, worth 1 to 7 points, and a Master Spy, worth 8 points. The idea is for each player to move his spies from their home territory into enemy home territory. The Master Spy must reach enemy HQ. On the way spies can challenge and capture enemy spies.

How to Play

Each player puts his spies on the red squares at his end of the board. Players move a spy one square each turn. Spies may only move diagonally but they can move either backwards or forwards.

Players may not miss a turn, but they do not have to challenge an enemy spy. To challenge, a spy must land on the square next to an enemy spy. The player then says 'I challenge you'.

The spy with the highest number wins and the loser goes off the board. If a spy challenges a Master Spy, the spy goes off the board and the player loses 10 points. If a Master Spy challenges another Master Spy, both stay on the board, but the challenger loses 10 points.

The game ends when one player has all his remaining men in enemy territory, and his Master Spy in the enemy HQ.

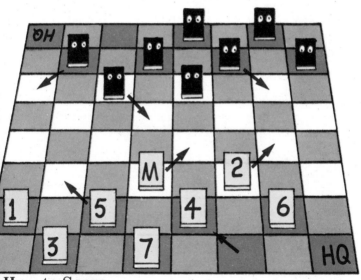

How to Score

Add up the numbers on your spies in enemy territory. Take away from your score any points you have lost during the game. The first person with all his remaining spies home and his Master Spy in enemy HQ adds 10 points. The player with the most points wins.

Spot the Spies

This game is a test of Good Spy disguises.
Two people can play or as many as you like.

All the spies arrange to be at one place, on one day, at a certain time. They can choose a main shopping street, a park or anywhere with lots of people. It helps the game if there is a clock at the chosen place.

Each spy then dresses up in a really Good Spy | disguise so no one will recognize them.

They go to the place at the right time and stay there for a certain time (that's why the clock is useful). They move about, | trying to spot the other spies but without being seen by them. A Good Spy always pretends he has a reason to be where he is.

Each spy carries a note book and a pencil. He writes down the names of each of the spies he spots and each bit of disguise they are wearing—a wig, a big black hat, padded stomach, a false moustache or big shoes.

Each spy also makes notes of what the other spies are doing. They might pretend to be shopping or delivering a parcel in the street. If it is in a park, they might pretend to feed the pigeons or fly a kite.

When the time is up, all the spies go home and take off their disguises. They then meet at the Good Spy Headquarters (if they have chosen one. Anywhere will do if they haven't). Each spy scores a point for every right bit of disguise and right bit of pretend action he has written down in his note book. He loses a point for every wrong bit written down. The spy with the biggest score is the winner. He is then called the Master Spy.

Which Hat?

A Good Spy may be sent on a secret mission at any time to anywhere in the world. He must wear the right clothes so he will not be noticed. Here is a Good Spy's hat cupboard.

Which hat or head-dress would he choose for these seven different places in the world? Look at the pictures and then decide on a hat. Check your answers at the bottom of the page.

Answers

1 A Russian fur hat
2 A Scottish tartan cap
3 A Mexican straw hat
4 An American cowboy hat
5 An Arab head cloth
6 A Swiss lady's lace cap
7 An Australian bush hat

Quick Disguise Collection

A Good Spy needs lots of clothes, bags, shoes, boots, hats, gloves, belts, scarves, walking sticks, umbrellas, sunglasses, spectacles and cheap jewellery. Collect as many different kinds as you can and keep them hidden in your secret disguise cupboard.

Try asking your family and their grown-up friends for old clothes and other things they do not want any more. Or you may be able to buy clothes and things very cheaply at old clothes sales or markets.

Get the clothes ready so you can put them on quickly when you need to disguise yourself. Put long clothes on hangers, if you can, so they do not get creased and crumpled. Clothes which are too big are useful because they change your shape and you can wear padding underneath.

Clothes Too Long

Cut off the ends of sleeves and trouser legs if they are too long. Snip round them as neatly as you can.

Cut off the ends of skirts and dresses. Turn the edges in and pin, glue or sew them up.

Stuff paper or bits of cloth into the toes of boots and shoes if they are too big. Or wear your own inside.

Ask a grown-up to take the glass out of old spectacles. Put rubber bands on the ends to stop them slipping.

Pin or sew old towels or rolled up material inside large coats—then the padding will not slip out.

Use belts on coats which are too big and to hold up trousers and skirts. They help to change your shape.

Check Your Equipment

When a Good Spy goes on a mission, he first checks that everything he wears or carries fits in with his disguise. If he says he comes from a certain country, his clothes, luggage, money, family photographs and letters must come from that country too. Here are some of the things a Good Spy checks and makes sure he has before he leaves his home base.

CUT OUT LABELS WITH MAKER'S NAME

TAKE EVERYTHING OUT OF POCKETS, BRIEFCASE OR HANDBAG

CHECK LABELS IN SHOES

A Good Spy cuts out all the labels from his clothes which might give him away – even shoes, boots and underwear.

He goes through his pockets and brief case. Then he puts in all the things that back up the man he pretends to be.

What to Take

A Good Spy writes himself letters addressed to the country he says he comes from, with the right stamps on.

He has a handkerchief with the initials of his false name in the corner. And a ball point pen with his false initials.

DIARY WITH FALSE NAMES AND PLACES

MONEY FROM HOME COUNTRY

NEWSPAPER CUTTING

NOVEMBER
30 Wallpaper at home

DECEMBER
1 Peter's birthday
2 Visit to

FAMILY PHOTOGRAPH

RED SPY SEEN IN TEA ROOM by

RAIL TICKET

BUS TICKET

STAMPS

A Good Spy gets his wallet ready very carefully. He collects things from the country he says he comes from.

And he writes up a diary, filling it in with the names of places he says he has been. This is useful if his story is questioned.

How to Put On Make-Up: 1

A Good Spy learns how to use simple make-up to change his looks. He can change his eyes, eyebrows and mouth easily and quickly with the sort of make-up grown-up women use. By carefully putting on shadows and lines, you can make your eyes seem bright or dull and your cheeks full, or hollow and old. You can also make yourself look ill or healthy.

Try putting on make-up in secret in front of a mirror. You need lots of light so that you can see what you are doing. Only use a little make-up to start with. It will show up much more in bright daylight than in electric light.

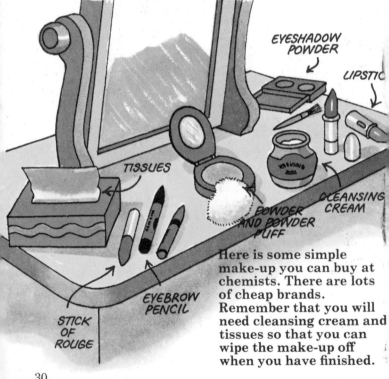

EYESHADOW POWDER

LIPSTIC

TISSUES

POWDER AND POWDER PUFF

CLEANSING CREAM

EYEBROW PENCIL

STICK OF ROUGE

Here is some simple make-up you can buy at chemists. There are lots of cheap brands. Remember that you will need cleansing cream and tissues so that you can wipe the make-up off when you have finished.

Eyebrows

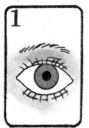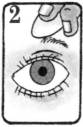

Use this easy trick to alter your eyebrows (1). First rub on thick white soap to blot them out (2).

Wait until the soap dries and they have disappeared (3). Draw on new eyebrows with a pencil (4).

Eyes

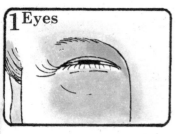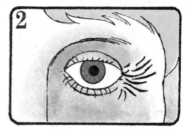

Screw up your eyes so you can see the wrinkles at each side of them. See how your eyelids crease.

Draw thin, dark lines with a soft eyebrow pencil along each crease. This makes you look older.

Baggy Eyes

The skin under some people's eyes hangs down in bags. Draw them with an eyebrow pencil.

Black Eye

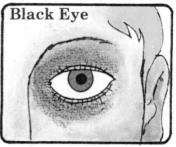

To pretend you have a black eye, brush blue and grey eye shadow round your eye. Smudge it a bit.

How to Put On Make-Up: 2

Here are some ways of making your face look older. Try using face powder to make it paler. Use dark eye shadow for the shadows. Do not forget to change your hair when you disguise yourself as an old person.

People's faces change as they grow older. Look at old people and you will see that their faces are often thin and pale. They have lines round their eyes and mouths, and their lips are thinner. They often have hollow cheeks.

Rub pale foundation cream over your lips until they are the same colour as the rest of your face.

Draw on a new, thin mouth with a very dark red lipstick. Make your lips look small and thin.

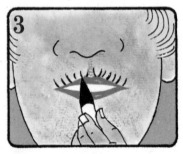

Old people often have wrinkled mouths. Draw thin lines round your mouth with a dark pencil.

Now make a face, pulling your mouth down at the corners. Draw dark lines where you see the creases.

1 Shadows

Look at your face to see where the hollows are. Feel it with your fingers to find the main bones.

2

Try brushing dark blue or grey eye shadow round your eyes. Shade it at the sides of your face.

3

Put dark powder shadows where there are hollows between the tops of your ears and your eyes.

4

Brush shadows on your cheeks below your cheek bones. This will make them look hollow.

5

Shadows each side of your nose make it look thin. Dab dark colour under your nose and mouth.

6

Use cotton wool to dab pale face powder over the parts of your face where there are no shadows.

33

Special Effects

Enemy spies will find it much more difficult to recognize you when you wear the sort of special effects shown on these pages. Do not use them too often or the Enemy Spies will soon get to know them.

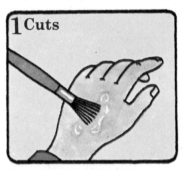

1 Cuts

2

Smear some Copydex on to your skin. As it dries, pinch the skin together to make it look like a cut.

Use red paint or felt tip along the lines of the cut. Then make dark stitch marks along each side.

1 Slings

2

3

4

You need a friend to help you make a sling like this. Fold a scarf or piece of cloth (1). Hold your arm across it, and put one end round your neck (2).

Lift the bottom end and knot it to the one round your neck (3). Once the sling is made, you can slip it on and off quickly to fool the Enemy Spies.

Black Teeth

Pretend you have lost some of your front teeth. Cut out small squares of gummed black paper and stick them on your teeth.

Eye Patch

Cut out a piece of card shaped like this. Paint it black on one side. Make holes at the top corners and tie on black elastic.

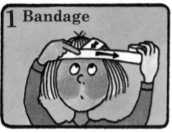

1 Bandage

Use a roll of bandage, or a long strip of ordinary white material. Begin with it rolled up.

2

Bind it as tightly as you can, then it will not slip. Fix the end with a safety pin, or tuck it in.

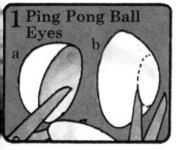

1 Ping Pong Ball Eyes

Cut a ping pong ball in half with scissors (a). Then cut a small, round hole in each half (b).

2

Colour the ping pong ball halves blue. Make small holes in each. Join with elastic to hold them on.

Change Your Walk

A Good Spy changes his walk to fit the disguise he is wearing. He knows he can easily be recognized in a crowd by the way he walks. Even if he is well disguised and even if the Enemy spies are too far away to see his face clearly, they may guess who he is.

Everyone moves their arms and holds their hands in certain different ways. This, too, can give away a good disguise, if it does not fit with a certain way of walking. Here are some walks for a Good Spy to practise.

Stiff Leg

Try walking with one stiff leg. Tie a scarf round one knee to make it difficult to bend.

Limp

Limp on one leg, walking as if it hurts. Put something in one shoe to remind you which leg it is.

Strutting

Walk quickly with your head up. Lean back and hold your hands behind you. Take big strides.

Slouching

Take small steps and shuffle your feet. Put your hands in your pockets and hunch your shoulders.

High-Heeled Totter

Wear high-heeled shoes
and take very small steps
Bend your knees and
bounce as you walk.

Low-Heeled Shuffle

Wear large flat shoes and
shuffle along, taking very
small steps. Lean forward
with your head down.

Toes In

Turn your toes in as you
walk. This makes you
move in quite a different
way. Lean forward a little.

Toes Out

Turn your toes out as far
as you can and bend your
knees. Put your feet down
flat and stamp a bit.

Striding

Walk quickly taking very
big strides, and swing
your arms. Put your heels
down first as you stride.

Bent Back

Bend sideways and put
your hand on that hip as
if you have a bad back.
Walk slowly.

Looking Fat

One of the best ways to disguise yourself is to change your shape. If you are thin, make yourself look like a fat person. Here are some hints on how to do it. Watch how fat people move and behave. This will give you lots of ideas for disguises, and hints on how to act as a fat, heavy person.

You can make your stomach look big by tying one or two cushions round your waist. Wrap a small towel round your shoulders to make them look broad. Tie scarves round your legs and arms to fill out your trousers and sleeves. Wear big clothes over your normal ones. Put on big shoes and gloves.

Fat People often look redder in the face than other people. Rub some rouge on your cheeks to make them red. Wear a high collar so your neck does not give you away.

A fat person gets out of breath easily. When pretending to be a fat person, puff and pant from time to time. Mop your forehead as if you are too hot.

A fat person will quite often lean slightly backwards to balance himself as he walks along. He may also stand with his feet wide apart for better balance.

Fat people usually move slowly and have some difficulty getting up and sitting down. They use their hands a lot to lower and raise themselves, especially in big chairs.

Looking Old

Disguising yourself as an old person is great fun. Remember that people change a lot as they grow older. Here are some things to think about when preparing your disguise.

Make yourself look like an old person by wearing clothes that are too big and are dull colours.

They should also look bulky and warm. Dark hats and scarves and glasses help the disguise.

An old person disguise is often useful on a secret mission. Knitting can be a good excuse for sitting and watching.

Old people are often a bit unsteady, so move slowly. Remember to hold on to things such as banisters when coming down stairs.

Most old people look friendly and innocent. A spy disguised as an old person should not be spotted by the Enemy.

Pretending to shop or look in shop windows is a good way of hiding in a group of people.

The disguise is also a good reason to walk slowly and stop often for a rest. This is useful when collecting information.

Old people often stoop a little. This makes them seem shorter. They shuffle their feet along and use walking sticks.

Pretend to be very stiff. Bending down slowly to pick something up off the ground is a good way to have a look around.

Secret Hiding Places: 1

A Good Spy often has to carry secret messages, films or documents from one place to another, or to give to his Contact. Some of these may be very small, but he will need secret hiding places in his clothes in case he is stopped and searched by Enemy Spies.

You can make secret pockets in your spy clothes. And there are lots of other places to hide small things in, so they are easy to get at when you want them.

1 Secret Pocket

Carefully cut a few stitches along the bottom of the lining of an old coat. Undo one side only.

2

Pull up the lining. Stitch a pocket, cut from an old coat, into the coat. Pull down the lining again.

1 Secret Slots

For this you need a wide belt. Cut a piece of thin card about 10 cm long and just thinner than the belt.

2

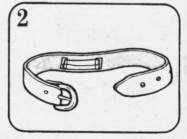

Stick the ends and bottom of the card to the inside of the belt. Use sticky tape or glue.

Wigs, hats, caps and berets

Put secret messages or letters on top of your head before you put on a wig. Fold them up first.

Bulky papers can go under a big hat. Hide smaller things, under a cap or in a beret.

Hat Bands

If you have to take your hat off, hide small messages behind the inside or outside band.

Collars

Tuck small messages under your collar. Push them up under the roll collar of a jersey.

Cuffs

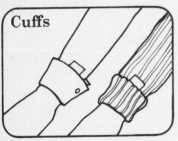

Messages can go inside folded cuffs of shirts or jerseys. They are easy to slip in and out.

Turn-Ups

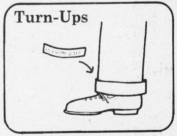

If you have turn-ups on your disguise trousers, roll up papers. Curve them to fit inside.

Secret Hiding Places: 2

1 Shoes

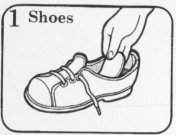

If you look inside most shoes you will find a thin inner sole. Pull up this sole from some old shoes.

2

Slide a secret message under the sole. Press it down. It will not show when the shoes are off.

Socks and Boots

Fold secret messages or papers into long thin strips. Slide them down your socks or long boots.

Tie

Look at the back of a tie. It has a fold all the way along. Slide a message in and pin it to the back.

Badge

Fold a secret paper very small. Stick it to the back of a badge or brooch with tape. Then pin it on.

Scarf

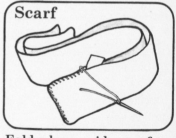

Fold a long, wide scarf lengthways. Sew up one end and part of one side. Slip in papers.

Newspaper

Slip large papers in a folded newspaper, magazine or comic. Carry it under your arm.

Record Sleeve

Slide large thin papers into a record sleeve. Push them well down. Carry the record sleeve openly.

1 Umbrella

Open a large umbrella. Roll secret papers round the handle. Put a rubber band round them to keep

2

them in place. Close the umbrella loosely to hide the papers. Remember them if it rains.

Guitar Case

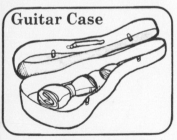

Carry very large bundles of secret papers in a guitar case. Or any instrument case will do.

Shopping Bag

Hide secret papers in the bottom of a shopping bag. Cover with fruit, vegetables, or groceries.

False Noses

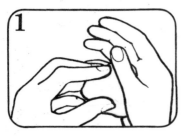

1

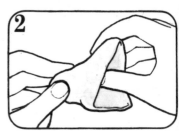

2

To make a false nose, use pale pink or pale brown plasticine. Knead it like this to make it soft.

Press the plasticine into a nose shape. Do not make it too big or it will be heavy and may fall off.

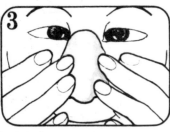

3

4

Press the nose over your own. Leave it open at the end so you can breathe. Smooth the edges down.

Shape the nose again. Hold up a second mirror so you see what you look like from the side too.

5

6

Rub make-up over your face and the new nose. Then they will both look the same colour.

If you think it might fall off, try putting on glasses. They will rest on the nose and hold it in place.

Hands and Nails

To make your hands look old, put blue or grey shadows on your fingers. Rub it between the joints.

You will see pale blue lines on the back of your hand. Draw on them with a blue pencil like this.

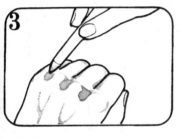

Now clench your fist. Rub blue pencil between your knuckles to make them look hollow.

Rub pale powder into your skin. This will make it look old and wrinkly. Dust it round your nails.

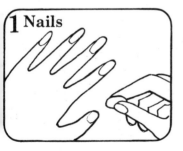

Cut ten nail shapes out of very thin white card. Stick them on your nails with quick-drying glue.

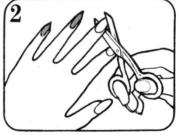

Trim the nails evenly. Paint them pink or red with water paint. Or try making different shapes.

47

Moustaches

Try making lots of different kinds and shapes
of moustaches to see which one suits you best.
Remember that moustaches, sideburns and
beards should all match the colour of your own
hair. Or your wig if you are wearing one.

The quickest way to give
yourself a moustache is
to draw or paint one

straight on to your skin.
Use a brown or black wax
crayon or eyebrow pencil.

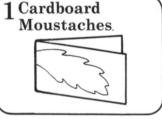

1 Cardboard Moustaches.

Fold a piece of card in
half and draw this outline
on the side of it. Cut it
out and paint it.

2

Wrap a piece of sticky
tape round your finger
with the sticky side out.
Slip it off and pinch it flat

3 *STICKY TAPE*

Stick one side of the
sticky tape to the back of
the moustache. Press it
on to your upper lip.

Wool Moustaches

For a more real-looking
moustache, stick wool on
to a card moustache or a
piece of stiff material.

Beards

Beards can be a very useful disguise if they look real, because they cover up so much of your face. Remember to check that they look right from the side and from the front.

Make this small goatee beard by sticking wool on to a triangle of fabric.

Thick sideburns made in the same way can make your face look different.

1 Bushy Beard

Bend some wire or joined pipe cleaners to hook over your ears. Join a loop to go round your mouth.

2 GLUE AND PINCH ALONG HERE

Lay a big piece of cotton wool over the wire frame. Fold it over and pinch it together with glue.

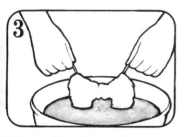

3

When the glue is dry, dip the beard in watery paint. Pull gently at the cotton wool to make it hairy.

4

Hang the beard up to dry by its wire ear hooks. Then it will be ready for use on your next mission.

49

Changing Your Hair

Another good way to change your appearance and make your disguise more real is to alter your hairstyle or make yourself a wig.

Brushing Back

If your hair usually falls forward over your forehead, try brushing it back with water.

Brushing Forward

If you usually brush your hair back or to one side, let it fall forward and hang over your eyes.

Change your Parting

See what happens if you change your parting from one side to the other. You may look quite different.

In the Middle

For a really funny look, part your hair down the middle. Even your friends may not recognize you.

Going White

A sprinkling of talcum powder will make your hair lighter. Wash or brush it out afterwards.

In the Net

If you have long hair, push it up into a hairnet. This will disguise both its length and its colour.

Wigs

1 Making a Wig

CUT-OFF
TIGHTS

OLD HAT

WOOLLY
BERET

If you want to make a full wig, you must first find a base that fits your head and covers your own hair.

This could be made from some cut-off tights, an old hat with the brim cut off, or a woolly beret.

Stick or sew strands of wool or untwisted string on to the base. Remember to start at the bottom.

Then the top layers will overlap the bottom ones. Now trim the hair to the style you want.

The Bald Look

The easiest way to make yourself look bald is to wear a plain pink bathing cap which covers up all your own hair. For a nearly-bald look, stick strands of wool round the sides of the cap.

Hats

Hats and scarves are useful disguises. Use them to hide part of your face or the shape of your head. Make a collection of different shapes and sizes. Always try to wear one that goes with the rest of your disguise.

All One Hat

Think of different ways of wearing the same hat or cap. Push it to the back of your head. Turn it round to face the back or try turning it inside out.

Bends	Shadows	Rain	Shine

Hats with wide brims are useful. Bend them into different shapes or hide your face in their shadow.

Choose your hat for a secret mission carefully. Do not be caught out by a change in the weather.

False Hair

1

2

Stick some strands of wool or string to the inside

of a hat or scarf. Use it to hide your own hair.

Scarves

Turbans

If you have a long scarf,
try making a turban.
Wind it round and round.
Then tuck the end in.

Scarves

Long scarves are also
very useful for hiding
most of your face from
the Enemy.

1 Tying a Headscarf

Here are three ways of
tying a square headscarf.
First fold it diagonally to
make a triangle.

2

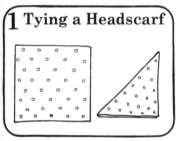

Lay the long edge over
your head. Tie two ends
under your chin. The third
corner hangs at the back.

3

Lay the long edge over
your head. Now take the
two front ends and tie
them at the back.

4

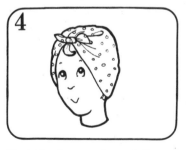

Put the long edge at the
back and a point at your
forehead. Tie the two
ends on top of your head.

Change Your Voice

One of the easiest ways to recognize someone is by the sound of their voice. However well you disguise your face or body, your voice may give you away.

If you want to disguise your voice by using a particular accent, you will have to practise it a lot before you talk to people. Foreign accents are fun but you must keep it up without speaking in your normal voice. Try talking in very high and very low voices as well.

1 On the Telephone

Hold a handkerchief over the mouthpiece. Ring up a friend who can tell you what you sound like.

2

Your voice will sound even more different if you screw up your lips as if you are about to whistle.

3

If you hold your nose while you are speaking, your voice will sound most peculiar.

4

Now give a big smile. Curl your lips back to show your teeth. Your voice will change again.

1 False Voices

The best ways of exposing a false voice are to make the suspect laugh or to give him a fright.

1 Who are you talking to?

If you need to pass a secret message, but you think you are being watched, don't look at the person you are talking to. Look at someone else or pretend to be doing something different.

Whispering

Practise whispering secret messages without moving your lips or looking at other people.

Try it in a public place such as a bus or train, until you can do it without anyone noticing.

Disguise Scrapbook 1

You can have fun making a scrapbook of ideas for different disguises and good places to spy. This will help you to build up a collection of clothes and equipment ready for secret missions. Cut out pictures from comics, magazines and travel brochures and stick them into your book.

When you plan a secret mission, remember that neither your disguise nor what you do should attract attention. You must plan to fit in with your surroundings. The next few pages will give you some ideas for spying on other people and buildings without being noticed.

Working Spies

A good time for spying, if you live in a town, is at rush hour in the morning or evening. There are always lots of people moving about carrying cases and reading papers.

No one has much time to notice anything else. If you are spying on a particular building, keep walking at the same pace as everyone else. Then come back again.

Summer Spies

Even on a very hot day on the beach, when no one wears many clothes, it is possible to spy without being seen. Wear a sun hat and dark glasses. Choose a spot where you can see in all directions.

Winter Spies

This is the easiest time for spying. Everybody is muffled up in warm clothes. You can bend your head and shuffle along without being noticed. Keep moving. No one stands still in the cold.

Bicycle Spies

A bicycle is a very useful piece of equipment for moving about and spying without being noticed.

Pretend your bicycle has a puncture. It is a good excuse to get off and keep watch on a building.

57

Disguise Scrapbook 2

1 Town Spies

Some places in town, such as bus stops, are good for spying. People are often waiting so you are less likely to be noticed by the Enemy.

2

Another good place is a railway station. There are always lots of people about when trains arrive. If you sit quietly, you may not be noticed.

Sleeping Spy

On a sunny day you can often see people asleep in parks and gardens. Are they asleep or spying?

Tourist Spy

No one suspects tourists of spying. They can stroll about taking pictures and looking at everything.

1 Country Spies

It is more difficult to spy in the country. You must have a good reason to be there, or you will look suspicious. Try pretending to be a bird-watcher.

2

Some secret buildings are in the country. Disguise yourself as a hiker. You can pretend to rest and read a map without looking suspicious.

Spy Pairs

Two people can often walk about happily together without arousing suspicion. A happy couple looks innocent.

Bad Spies

Bad spies look obvious. Never pace up and down impatiently. People will wonder who you are.

Spy Spotter's Sketchbook: 1

A Good Spy finds it very useful to be able to draw people's faces. Then he can keep a record of what Enemy Spies look like. The different parts of a face, such as eyes, nose and ears are called features. The next four pages show you how to draw people's faces and where the features go.

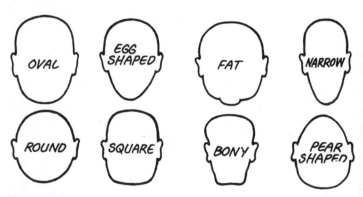

Head Shapes

Everybody's head is a different shape. Use these head shapes to copy or trace. Choose the one you think is most like the person you want to draw.

Where Features Go

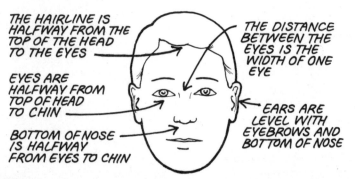

THE HAIRLINE IS HALFWAY FROM THE TOP OF THE HEAD TO THE EYES

EYES ARE HALFWAY FROM TOP OF HEAD TO CHIN

BOTTOM OF NOSE IS HALFWAY FROM EYES TO CHIN

THE DISTANCE BETWEEN THE EYES IS THE WIDTH OF ONE EYE

EARS ARE LEVEL WITH EYEBROWS AND BOTTOM OF NOSE

LARGE WIDE-OPEN EYES WITH BUSHY EYEBROWS.

SMALL DEEPSET EYES.

SLANTING-DOWN EYES AND EYEBROWS

SLANTING-UP EYES AND EYEBROWS

Eyes and Eyebrows

Here are four different pairs of eyes. Eyes are difficult to draw because you need to get really close to people to see their shape and colour.

LONG AND THIN

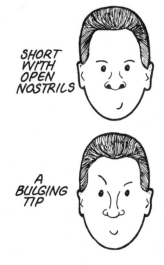

SHORT WITH OPEN NOSTRILS

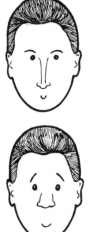

SHORT AND FLAT

A BULGING TIP

Noses

These pictures show what different shaped noses look like from the front.

On the next page you can see how to draw them from the side as well.

Spy Spotter's Sketchbook: 2

When you look at a face from the side, it is called a profile. A good disguise can easily change someone's face from the front, but it is much more difficult to hide the shape of features in profile. Here are some things to look out for when drawing faces from the side.

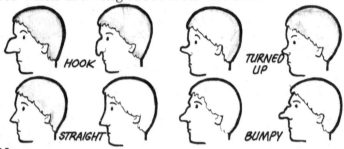

Noses

Noses are difficult to disguise in profile. They stick out and there are many different shapes.

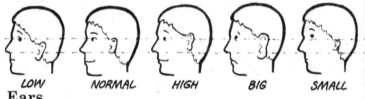

Ears

The tops of most people's ears are on a level with their eyes. Ears are usually twice as long as they are wide. There are many different shapes.

Chins

These pictures show what the same man would look like with different chins.

No disguise would hide a big chin, except a real or false beard.

Hair

These pictures show how the same man can make himself look completely different. He just changes the style and length of his hair or wears a wig.

Beards

Beards and moustaches are some of the most often used disguises. So it is important to learn to draw them and notice how they change a face.

Hats and Glasses

Here is the same man again looking quite different in each picture.

Would you guess he was the same man as the one in the top row?

Spy Language

Agent—A spy.

Briefing—A meeting when spies are given information and instructions about an assignment.

Bug—A very small microphone hidden in a room so that people talking in the room can be overheard, and perhaps recorded, outside.

Classified Information—Information that is so secret that only certain people are allowed to know about it.

Courier—A spy who carries orders or messages.

Headquarters (H.Q.)—The place, perhaps secret, a spy ring operates from.

Impostor—A spy who is disguised to look like, and pretends to be, another person.

Master Spy—The head of a spy ring.

Opposition—The enemy.

Set-up—A trap to catch an Enemy Spy.

Spy Ring—A group of spies or agents.

Surveillance—Keeping watch secretly on an Enemy Spy, or on a building which Enemy Spies use as their H.Q. or as a Rendezvous.

Suspect—A person suspected of being a spy.

Undercover Agent—A spy operating in disguise in enemy territory.